Angel

DEDICATION

This novel is dedicated to all those readers who love adventure, angels, God, Jesus and for those who are unable to join us due to severe illness or death defying sickness!

"For God so loved the world that He gave his only begotten Son, that whosever believeth in Him shall have everlasting life."

"Our Father who art in heaven, hallowed be thy name, thy kingdom come, thy will be done on earth as it is in heaven. Please give us this day our daily bread and lead us not into temptation, but deliverth us, for thine is the kingdom, the power, and the glory forever and forever!"

ABOUT THE AUTHOR

The author and his wife, Joyce, grew up and spent a good part of their lives in Yakima, Washington, going to work and attending school. Their High School year was full of happiness. It was pure bliss!!!

Roy and Joyce, were married on August 12, 1961, in the Baptist Church on Yakima Avenue. He was later baptized there. They were 19 years old when they married. She, Joyce, was only 14 years old as a Junior High School student. Joyce's mother had, ironically, the last name of Cantrell, the same as Joyce's married name. She was 24 when she gave birth to a baby boy named Steven Kent. He was born on December 31, 1966, in a hospital at a town called Tacoma, Washington. Joyce was 18 when she graduated from A. C. Davis Senior High School in June of 1960.

Roy worked first at Paine Field, Everett, Washington and then at McChord Air Force

Base, Tacoma, Washington. He was an Air Force man with 21 years, 9 months, and 29 days of military service. Roy started on as a Federal Civil Service employee beginning work on May 6, 1963. He was hired as an Air Force Reserve Technician with a military grade being at Staff Sergeant, E-5. His job came with a requirement to be a Records' Clerk, then a Testing and Classification Specialist, and later an Air Force Reserve Recruiter at grade Master Sergeant, E-7. He was recalled to extended active duty in January of 1968.

Roy's father was a hard-working man who worked for the Northern Pacific railroad. He worked for the Northern and Missouri Pacific Railroads for over 25 years. Roy's mother was a hardworking housewife and a mother of 11, six boys and five girls. One boy passed away at 3, one baby girl, a twin of Leo Edwin, died at birth. He was born on his mother's birthday. She was named Estella and she married William Lockwood of Missouri. She was born on February 27, 1898, in Pleasanton, Kansas. William, Bill, was born in Joplin, Missouri. His date of birth was June 27, 1899.

Steven was born on December 31, 1966, and is the father of a girl, our grand-daughter, Jacqueline (Jackie) Marie, and a boy, our grandson, Brian James. He and his wife, Barbara K., were married in Aurora, Colorado.

Steve and Barb work for Federal Civil Service. He as an Army Explosive Ordinance Specialist. She as an Accountant. Brian works as a Stocker or a Store Clerk. He is attending college. Jackie works as an Accounting Technician/Specialist for the Department of the Army.

Roy is an Author, Artist, who is just beginning to write novels and non-fiction books. He has written: "By the Grace of God", "Destiny", "Angel", and "Satire." The last one is yet to be written. Several of his books came from dreams, such as Angelica Marie Angel! Sequels will follow especially since Destiny Never Ends!

Artist: Jacqueline Marie Cantrell

Jomast B

An Ode to My Angel

Michael Cassi

Fly me to your heavenly garden of peace
With your pure and perfect pallid wings
Carry me to my fairest hopes and dreams
And put my feet up on your red roses bed.

Bless my mornings with your comforting
touch
And feed me with your sweetest smiles
I'll drink your tears to heal my pains
And live with you forevermore.

Guide me to my future successes
With your eyes so angelic and divine
Sing your most romantic melodies
Erase my worries and perplexities.

O my dearly beloved angel of heavens
Your smell I breathe awakens me
Embrace me with your warmest arms
Forever I will live with thee.

CHAPTER 1: THE END

September 5, 2000

"So, this is how it ends, huh?" Matt thinks with a mix of self-pity and anger; the red-hot, molten lava anger that was threatening to burn his heart and flow out of his 6 feet, 1 inch, muscular body.

He had woken up earlier than usual and looked at his wife on the other side with her back to him. That gesture summed up the massive challenges both were experiencing in their relationship. "Where has all the love gone?" It would have been easier to place the blame on someone if his wife had cheated on him. His honest attempts to save their 15-year marriage were as fruitless as a Japanese stone garden. If going to numerous marriage counselors proved anything it was that he knew he couldn't open up to anyone anymore, not his wife, not the Harvard-educated therapists, not his parents even.

The sound of the alarm, screaming at 5:55 am was unbearable; it was if it was announcing to the whole world that his marriage was quickly coming to a screeching halt.

Aaghh!

He hung his head down as if admitting defeat and then got himself up to get ready for work. As the president of a construction company in Akron, Colorado, he had to make sure he got to his client's construction project before all his sub-contractors. "No point in dragging the sadness of my personal life into my career," he said to himself as he aggressively zipped-up his jacket to create a buffer between his body and January 2nd's 16°F.

"Dad!" he heard his 11-year old daughter, Stacy, call after him as he was rushing to get out of his 2 car garage. He couldn't help but smile. His daughter was his stress ball. No matter how much stress was jammed into his jaw or shoulders, one thought of Stacy would melt it away in a jiffy.

"Dad, can I have $20? Emma and I will be going to the book fair at the school."

"Sure, sweetie, here, take $40."

"No, no, I don't need $40! Just $20!"

"You must the world's only kid in the world who refuses to let her dad spoil her. What are you going to buy?"

"Harry Potter and the Goblet of Fire."

"OK. Tell mom to pick you up from school as I will be working late today."

"Ok." Stacy went back inside and Matt started his truck. Throughout his drive his mind was playing his marriage's happy moments like a projector as if trying desperately to find something that he could use to extend into his current life and erase the bleak and cold relationship his marriage had been reduced to.

"Stupid!" he heard someone scream at him as he was about to hit a jaywalker. At any other time in his life, he would have been offended and lashed out with his choicest curses reserved for careless street crossers, but today was different. "That must be a wakeup call for me," he thought. "Wake up call? From what? Is it really time to acknowledge that the marriage is really over between me and my high-school sweetheart?" Actually, he had loved Miranda ever since he knew her from Middle School. "Was I foolish to marry her? I did get at least 14 wonderful years out of this marriage, so it must not be a total failure."

He had to stop his train of thoughts when he reached 805 E 4th St, headquarter of his small construction company, Quigley Construction Co., Today was the 15th

Angel

anniversary of his company. Unlike his marriage, his business was good. Each year, he was experiencing 27% growth and with the advent of Internet, he was positioned well to market his company online. None of his competitors had a website yet and he was determined to make sure he covered that gap and was already starting to feel the benefit of his $10,977 investment. His business partner, Parker, had been skeptical at first about investing in a media that was so new.

"I'd rather prefer that you invest that in sponsorships like we did 7 years ago." Parker's high pitched voice echoed back.

"Didn't you see the ROI? We got only two new projects through that. Parker, I know you are apprehensive about this considering the dot-com bubble, but trust me on this, will ya? I am willing to sign a document that if this is a complete failure, then I will not take this year's bonus, ok?"

Parker shook his head in a no then a yes.

"All right, now come on before we are late for this morning's meeting." Parker hopped into Matt's GMC truck as his tire squealed to rush to their meeting.

"Slow down, Matt!" Parker screamed as his coffee threatened to spill over his new silk tie.

"Wasn't that your wife's present for you last year?"

"Yes, our 25th wedding anniversary gift," Parker said fondly making Matt suck in his guts with stress over his not-so-great marriage.

"Oh!" Matt exclaimed as he nearly hit a young woman with hair that looked as it was shining from inside, like fiber optic filaments. No time to waste he regretfully had to pry his eyes away and pay attention to the road.

"That would have been a shame if you had hit that girl" Parker chuckled.

Thankfully, the rest of the 16-minute ride to their project's site was uneventful.

***

"Matt! Good to see you! Sorry, I couldn't talk more at our last meeting."

"No worries, Pat. I understand." Matt shook his client's hand firmly. Pat was one of his ideal clients. Paid bills on time and was receptive to Matt and Parker's ideas. Sadly, very few in their client base were like that and they really were the 80 of the 80-20 rule.

Pat smiled and nodded, "Let's get started with our meeting." The three sat down at the large meeting table.

***

When the meeting ended, Parker and Matt got back in their company truck to head to their headquarter.

"So, will you let the accountant know that we have hired another sub-contractor and that he needs to add him to our payroll?"

"Aren't you going to...LOOK OUT!"

All Matt heard was a crashing sound as his truck got hit by a tractor-trailer coming from the right lane and lost its control.

The truck bounced and flew over two cars before hitting a tree in on the left side of the road. Matt lost consciousness but Parker, although badly injured was conscious enough to get out of the truck and inspect the damaged. The truck was totaled. He was more worried about his partner than their truck and didn't notice that a woman and few other people were starting to crowd around the truck.

"Someone please call an ambulance!" Parker yelled as loud as he could.

The woman examined Matt vitals and with the help of two other strangers were able to pry him safely out of the truck and start CPR.

When cops and ambulance arrived on the scene, Matt was just starting to regain consciousness. The paramedics started their standard battery of questions. Being coherent, he emphatically said, "I don't want to go, I don't need to go" but they took him anyway.

Sigh.

"Might as well relax and let this whole charade of nonsense unfold in front of me." Matt thought and then felt the warmth of a hand on his right arm prompting him to look to the right and saw the face of the same woman that had hair that looked like it was lit from inside. He laid there agape, as paramedics wheeled him away into the ambulance. After that, everything went dark again.

***

When Matt opened his eyes he felt sore and stiff. He was alone on a hospital bed.

"Hello?!"

In a few seconds, a friendly face of a nurse popped in. "How do you feel, honey?

"Like crap. Like a bull dozer had rolled all over me and crushed my bones to pieces."

"Well, you are lucky to be alive. Here take these."

"What are they for?

"Pain."

"Is anything seriously wrong with me?"

"No, after that accident, you did get a whiplash and your muscles will be sore for a few days.

"Where's my family?"

"They have been called and your wife will be here in a few minutes. But, like I said, you are lucky."

"How soon can I be discharged?"

"As soon as your family can get you."

When Miranda arrived at the hospital, Matt was surprised that she genuinely looked worried about him. "Does she care about me?" He thought.

***

Even though Miranda had been very helpful in getting Matt back in shape to go back to work, he was not convinced that their marriage was what it used to be: intimate. Not just sexual intimacy, but also emotional and spiritual intimacy. He loved sharing his thoughts about God, Jesus and what it meant to be Christian with her and she loved sharing about what her faith, Judaism, meant to her. All of that sharing was gone, buried under years of boring routines of working, cooking, paying bills, day in, day out. "Maybe if I can outsource the boring parts of our lives, would that help me revive our relationship?" A fleeting though passed by Matt's mind which got brushed away when the door bell distracted him. It was the next door neighbor, Heather, she wanted to make sure that Miranda was still going to the "Girls Night Out" that night. A shade of jealousy hovered over Matt, making him feel more isolated and he withdrew even more.

It took three weeks for Matt to get over the soreness and stiffness from his truck accident.

"Parker, I think we need to boost marketing and consider joining our local Chamber again."

"Good, that will get you back in the loop. When are you thinking of renewing the membership?"

"This Thursday as they have an evening networking event I want to attend. You should attend it too; will be good to multiply our networking efforts."

"I'll put that on my calendar. What time?

"7 pm."

"I'll see you there at 6:30 pm, then."

"Ok. Oh and do bring Marcee as well. I think she is great at business networking for our company."

"Will do. What about Miranda?"

"Hmm, nah. Not this time."

***

Matt had to park his new Lexus GS300 half a mile away from the Chamber event. Dressed in sports coat fashioned from pure

Italian virgin wool and framed with smart notch lapels, Matt looked very handsome. He stepped out and turned around to go towards the entrance.

"Hi!"

Matt turned backward, towards the voice and felt as if someone had hit him with an electric bolt and at the same time a giant wave of fresh air from Paradise wafted towards him, threatening to seize his breathing. It was the same girl with neon hair that he had seen twice so far.

"How are you doing?" she walked towards him and he felt as if she was not walking on Earth but floating on a heavenly cloud.

He wanted to talk but nothing was coming out to his throat. He cleared his throat and said," I am fine...Uhhh, please forgive my manners, my name is Matt and I am very sorry that I was almost going to hit you that day...." he was stuttering and felt embarrassed.

"No to need to apologize. Then I saw you in that terrible accident. How are you now?"

"Much better," he managed to utter even though his throat was as dry as freeze dried strawberries. So, that's why he saw her that time when he was being wheeled into the ambulance!

"There you are!" Parker's high-pitched voice made both turn in his direction. Parker's face was astonished to the same woman he saw at their accident scene. "You are that same girl! Matt, I forgot to tell you that before the ambulance whisked you away, this young lady is responsible for saving your life."

Matt gave both a face that said, "what are you talking about?!"

The girl just smiled, allowing Parker to finish telling him. "She did the CPR on you."

"Ohhhh!" Long pause, then, "thank you so much. . . I am flabbergasted!! I don't even know your name . . ."

"I am Angelica," she said with a shy smile.

"Please, can we get inside, my hot cocoa is getting cold here!" Parker complained and everyone walked briskly towards the entrance of the building, grateful for the warmth inside.

***

"So..." Matt nodded and looked deeply in Angelica's eyes and said,' you are the person I need to thank for saving my life."

Angelica shook her head, "I just did what anybody would have done."

"Aww, please do not be so humble! Let me get you a drink."

Throughout the networking event, Matt couldn't shake the feeling off as if Angelica thought he was the most important person in that room full of at least 150 people.

"Is she flirting with me or she just friendly?" He thought to himself but realized that he was talking out loud when Parker responded, "who are you talking about?" Startled, he couldn't hide his thoughts from his best friend and business partner. Saving his buddy embarrassment of having to say it verbally, Parker, looked towards Angelica and raised his eyebrow as a sign language for a question. Matt nodded.

"I know what you are going through. . . I think she is a very friendly person." Parker attempted to assuage Matt's restless heart and Soul. Matt nodded but wasn't convinced.

An Ode to My Angel

Artlantica

You're like a flower

Sweet and beautiful all the way

Your beauty and charm

Seems like out of this world

Your eyes and your smile

Your heart and your soul

All I was looking for all my life is you

No one else but you

All I need is you

By my side

All I'm thinking of is you

All day and night

You're all I need

You're all I love

I love you the way you are

Love you more than anything else

You're my angel, you're my inspiration

You mean everything to me

You're the one I was looking for all my life

Yes, all my life

All I need is you

By my side

All I'm thinking of is you

All day and night

You're all I need

You're all I love

All I need is you

By my side

All I'm thinking of is you

All day and night

You're all I need

You're all I love

You're all I need

You're all I love

CHAPTER 2: TEMPTATION

It was hard for Matt to leave the Chamber event and the only factor he could put a finger on was Angelica. Could that be the factor that was destroying his marriage? The desire of feeling of being in love? That heady feeling you get when you first start falling in love?

"Oh Lord!" he blurted and realized that he was in his bedroom and his wife was sleeping next to him. At age 33, that's all he needed to derail his comfortable family life.

He needed to brush that off and get back to try to sleep and gaze at his wife's back.

They used to have a fairly decent romantic life; they got engaged when still in High School and then married after graduating. At that time, life was exciting, Miranda was exciting. There is a whole new horizon to explore. He loved seeing his new bride in sexy negligees and learn about Kama Sutra, Tantra, Yoni Eggs . . . Then the kids came along. First Rory. Then Stacy came along exactly 3 years later, then they had baby Billy; bouncy, epitome of 'babyness': cute, chubby and giggling and laughing at everything and anything.

So when exactly did love start to leave our nest? After baby one, two or three?

Maybe there was no genuine love to begin with?

"Yeah, go right ahead, Mr. Quiggly," he heard a voice in his head, "your glass is not just half empty, it has always been completely empty." With that defeating thought, Matt chest sunk in as if someone had punched him in the heart and ripped it out as well.

He tried to go back to sleep so he decided to go to his home office and update his Work Planner. Passing a cursory look over his weekly calendar, he focused on next morning. He had 45 minutes free before lunch. A vision of him having lunch with Angelica passed by, taking his breath away.

"Why not?" and then he wrote down to call her in the morning to see if he could convince her to have lunch with him.

Sigh.

Feeling better, he got back in bed as quietly as he could, as a disturbing picture his conscience screaming at the top of its voice, announcing to the world, "Alert! Alert! Mr. Quiggly is about to commit adultery!" The truth was, he was feeling guilty that he was thinking more of Angelica than his wife. He startled when his wife turned around and asked, "can't sleep?"

"Aagh! You scared me! No Hon, having trouble staying asleep. Sorry if I woke you up."

"No, you didn't. I thought I heard Billy calling me, so I went and checked on him. He was asleep." Miranda brushed with the back of her nails, the hollow in her neck. The same gesture that would drive Matt mad and have an urge to sweep her in his arms. Now it just made his heart feel heavy knowing that they were drifting apart, slowly but surely. He nodded as if acknowledging his thoughts.

"Huh?" Miranda startled him again. "Did I miss anything?"

"Oh, no, I was just thinking of something and accidently nodded. You go back to sleep, Hon. I'll try to catch a few winks myself before the morning."

Miranda reached out and touched his arm, then quickly withdrew at the awkwardness of that touch. It felt like they were strangers. Their eyes crossed guiltily at each other and then their backs to each other, pretending to sleep.

***

The morning was a refuge for Matt; to get out of the house, away from the marital breakdown he was witnessing every day. It was as if he was watching Mount Everest crumble down in slow motion, one chip of stone falling away at a time.

"Ugghh!" he wanted to scream as loud as he lungs could but his surroundings were not compatible with his needs; stuck in the morning's rush hour. He made a mental note of planning a camping trip to the woods; then he might get a chance to scream as much as he wanted to. He would be able to cry and complain to God that why was his marriage dissolving like this and why he was not able to do anything about it. Why was he just a silent spectator, rather than a proactive husband, feeling connected with his wife and lover?

When he got to his office, he couldn't wait to call Angelica. He had it all planned out: what, when, where. He grabbed the phone and dialed. It was a different story when she picked up the phone.

"I. . .I . . .Hi, Angelica? This is Matt! Good, good. I am good, thank you and you? Listen, I don't want to take too much of your time early in the morning. Would you join me for lunch today at Biaggi's? Yes, the new location. 12:30 will work for you? Good. I'll be there." Feeling like a High Schooler asking for a date, he put the receiver of the phone down with shaky hands. Then cupped his hands and breathed into them as if trying to revive himself to life. That's right, he was trying to chase life as he knew it; full of love and excitement.

Now Matt could concentrate on his work. The restlessness melted away into a soothing, meditation-like calm focus. Soon it was 12 noon and he jumped out of his chair, grabbed his jacket and flew away in his new truck. It really felt like his truck had grown a pair of wings. Traffic was unusually little at that time. He was able to get to the restaurant earlier than planned and asked for a table for two.

"No, not that one. Can we get one in the back there?"

"Sure," the petite waitress spun around and led him to the table in the back. "I am Becky and I will be serving you. Can I get something for you to drink while you wait?"

"Yes, Perrier with a lemon slice, please?"

The waitress nodded and scurried away.

As soon as he was about to sit down, Angelica came towards him. He got up to give her a hug.

"Thank you for accepting my invitation." he tried to make eye contact with her and she did the same. He tried to read her eyes. Will she flirt with me again? He hoped she would.

"Thank you for inviting me, " she said in her soft-spoken voice. "So what do you have on your mind?" She didn't waste much time, he thought.

The question caught him off guard as he didn't plan what he will be talking about with her? The trusty stuttering habit returned to save the day. "I . . .I . . . wanted to learn more about the project you said you were working on . . ."

"The Veteran's memorial project?"

He nodded.

"Well, sadly it has come to a stop; it is getting stalled because we cannot find anyone qualified to do the etching part.

"Is it acid etching?

"As a matter of fact, it is. Do you know anyone?"

"As a matter of fact, I do," and smiled like a well-fed cat.

She chuckled. "Ok, can you introduce them to me? Or send their contact details via email?"

"Yes, actually I have their business card in my truck. I'll give it to you before you go back to your office."

She nodded and the waitress came back to ask, "You two ready to order"

Both nodded.

"I'll have Salmon with Bourbon Sauce, please." Angelica said in her shy voice, emphasizing the 'please'.

Waitress turned towards Matt and he ordered the same as Angelica, even though Bourbon sauce didn't sound very appetizing to him.

Their orders came 9 minutes later and they conversed about trivial stuff. They went through their lunch quickly, shook hands with promises to touch base on the etching project.

***

As promised, Matt called his etching contact and requested him to call Angelica as soon as possible. Then the next day he asked if they had connected with each other yet and how it all went. Smiling to himself that he got another chance to contact Angelica, he dialed her number with fingers that wanted to dance with joy.

"Hi, Angelica! How are you? I wanted to find out if you are happy with Brian, the etching professional? Great! That's good to hear."

"Matt, there's a possibility that Mr. Leightly, our company's President will be considering hiring another construction company. There are several grievances against the current contractor we were working with. Is it ok if I give your contact details to him?"

"Sure!" Matt said very loudly. "Sorry to hear that your company is having trouble, but I will be happy to help if I can. "

"OK, then I'll call you if he asks to meet you."

Matt was thrilled that he didn't have to come up with an excuse to call her again; this time she will hopefully be calling him.

He didn't have to wait long for Angelica to call. She called the next day. "Mr. Leightly is eager to meet you and your partner, what's his name, oh yeah, Parker."

"Great! Would he like to come by and meet us or would he prefer we come to your office?

"If you two can come here to meet him, that would be great. Bring any portfolio materials you have and I can have Rita, our Administrative Assistant call you to set up a meeting. OK?"

"OK"

Hanging up the phone, he opened up his calendar and called Parker.

"Parker, there is a possibility of getting a new contract. Mr. Leightly of Leightly Media is looking for a new construction company."

"You mean Larry Leightly?"

"Yes.

"That would be great if we can do a project for them. When is the meeting?

"I will be getting a call from his Assistant to request a meeting. I have your calendar with me so can I give them 10 am on tomorrow which is Tuesday or 9:30 on Wednesday?

"Yes, that will be fine."

***

Rita, Mr. Leightly's Assistant called right after he hung up with Parker. He liked doing business at the speed of thought. They set up a meeting for 9 am on Tuesday. Parker would be able to come at 9:30 am.

The next day couldn't have come fast enough for Matt. Parker was able to come earlier and Matt was grateful for his support for landing this important project. He was very anxious to find out more about this project as well as Mr. Leightly. Beside owning the TV station, he also owned several media companies in Colorado.

The meeting went like a gentle wind from a heaven; everything just glided like they had rehearsed this a hundred times. Parker had brought in a mini-projector to share their portfolio and Mr. Leightly was delighted with their accomplishments. They were thrilled that they will be completing the $3.6 million project involving building a memorial garden for veterans.

The next day Matt called Angelica to thank her for helping him get a wonderful client.

"Angelica, it would be an honor if you can have lunch with me again. How about The Melting Pot?"

"Jeez, that is very pricy for a simple business lunch, Matt." Angelica protested.

"Nah. That's the least I can do as a 'thank you' for helping me get introduced to Mr. Leightly."

"OK. Let's meet today at 12 noon. OK?"

"Ok. See ya then."

***

He got to the Melting Pot, 5 minutes earlier. Angelica was right on time and sat opposite him.

"Congratulations again, Matt. You and Parker made quite an impression on Mr. Leightly. "

Matt felt like a Cheshire cat, grinning as widely as he could manage.

After their drinks and orders were taken care of. Matt cleared his throat and looked at Angelica.

"I didn't ask you here today for a business matter, Angelica."

"Oh?" Angelica chuckled, "what do you have on your mind then?" She flicked a strand of her hair and looked into his eyes, trying to match the seriousness of Matt's facial features. He reached over, gently, caressing her fingers.

"I have a personal favor to ask."

"Oh no!" she chuckled again and then tried to regain her serious look, without much success.

"I am going through a difficult time in my marriage and seriously considering separating from my wife and I . . .I am looking for a new partner," Matt blurted out without beating around the bush, making Angelica bite her lower lip.

She nodded slowly and then asked," I can empathize. What or how can I help? " She knew exactly what he was talking about but feigned not knowing about it.

"I know you are single and I feel very strongly. . . that you will be the perfect partner for me."

Angelica gasped and put a hand on her heart and then burst out laughing and looked furtively to make sure she didn't disturb the peaceful ambiance of the restaurant.

"Matt! Well, I was hoping you will at least woo me. But, I am afraid I will not be the right partner for you."

"Give me one good reason, why not?"

"Well, because. . . for one, I am. . .not a human."

Matt blinked repeatedly, then shook his head and said, "excuse me? that is the most absurd thing I have ever heard! You can be direct with me, Angelica. If you do not want to be with me, I can understand"

Angelica held up her hand to request ceasing all protests from Matt and then stood up. Matt thought she was walking away, instead she turned around and walked through a wall and came back as fast a flash.

Matt gulped hard and reached for his drink. Instead, he spilled it all over his clothes and the table. He was shaking by the time Angelica sat down. She put her hand on his gently and his shivering stopped. She was surprised that he didn't pass out.

"I am sorry, Matt. If I was made of flesh and blood, you would be a great partner for me."

Matt felt warmth rolling down his cheek. No! That could not happen to me! He could hear his mind screaming.

Angelica wiped his tear away. "I knew the trouble in your marriage before you knew me." She held his hands in hers.

Matt felt like a 7-year-old being comforted by his Mom when he had come home feeling defeated from a bullying experience on a school bus. The words poured out of him, "I feel so lost. I want to save my marriage, but I feel like running away . . ."

"So it can solve itself?" Angelica finished the sentence for him. They must have sat there for 45 minutes before the waitress came back with a bill.

"Will it be ok if I call you tomorrow morning? I have some news for you." She said.

Matt nodded gently, still feeling defeated.

Angelica then laid her right hand on his heart and he could feel the pain receding. It only took 2 seconds but he felt as if she had healed what was ailing him and his marriage.

"Listen, Angelica, thank you for listening, I feel it helped tremendously, as a matter of fact, I think I know what I need to do rebuild a relationship with my wife." Feeling renewed sense of energy surging through his heart and Soul, he gave Angelica a friendly hug. "Oh, I forgot to tell you why this veteran memorial project means so much to me."

"Oh, so it is not just the money?" Angelica smiled and winked.

"Ha ha, well that is nice too, but it means so much to be able to honor our veterans here. You know, I have an uncle that I have never met. He disappeared during World War II. "

"Hmm, what's his name?"

"John Quiggly"

"I might be able to help. I'll call you tomorrow with more details if I can."

"OK. Thanks."

My Angel

Veronica Mendoza

the stars are in your eyes

the moon is in your lips

the sun is in your skin

it makes you glow...

just like an angel....

the angel in my heart

you keep it together

when it starts fall apart.

cause your my angel..

my guardian angel...

your there through it all...

you catch me when i fall..

you never leave me behind

Angel

you're there waiting with me

no matter the time...

CHAPTER 3: THE FRIENDLY GUIDE

Angelica "Angel" Marie, at 5'6", 128 pounds, blue eyes, shiny blond hair is, to say the least, extremely gorgeous. Her attire is simple in design and consist of Beige nylons, a very shiny light tan in color, a black, silky, garter belt, and 4" black high heels or shiny black slippers.

Although she doesn't wear makeup, but if somebody tried to recreate the effect, it would require Channel Number 5, light fluffy rouge, eyebrow black covering and beautiful red lipstick. A blue, black, or red ribbon with a very pretty bow in her gorgeous hair. A smooth, clear, face with a nose and ears that were also clear and smooth. With jewelry being small, she wears pierced ear rings and a small, Pearl necklace with a 20" gold chain and, occasionally a small, but beautifully shaped ruby broach or pendant.

Angel lives with a roommate, named Mary Elizabeth some 200,000 miles to the North of the Gates of Heaven. Angel and her neighbors share just about everything. They are all located 75,000 miles from each other. Angel and her fellow Angels take turns supporting themselves and others. They usually have 35 clients each. Their island is seven miles long and eight miles wide.

In her past life, Angelica lived a life of a young mother with excruciatingly poignant lifestyle, which helped her learn to be empathetic, a skill very much useful in the non-human form. When not busy with helping her clients, she often spends time in the ethereal library of the Heaven, to hone her skills to help her clients.

When she was new to her non-human form, she sought the help of Aaroon, the Lord of the Library to help her get acquainted on how to access information from the Books that were holographic. Once she got the hang of it, knowledge and wisdom, would effortlessly download in to her being.

She was assigned her responsibilities directly by God as well as Jesus, with her current key responsibility being helping Matt and his family leading a positive, happy and healthy life, making a positive impact to their community. She loved being able to spend time with Jesus, who she had admired and loved event when she was in human form.

Angelica loved studying the planets and stars in the Universe, how they were made, why they were formed and their ecosystems. A few times she even taught Astronomy at an University.

Her favorite 'job' once she had was teaching International Affairs and this was an excellent opportunity to shape the minds of the young thinkers with positive and life-changing thoughts. This gave her a chance to teach about world problems that are currently plaguing our World: poverty, lack of education, illnesses.

She understood how such a trivial job could have long-term repercussions and be able to reach World Leaders. The result of her effort was that World Leaders convened in Geneva and began the very difficult task of discussing the World's prominent problems. The first task concerned eradicating hunger and extreme shortage of food in the Middle East and Africa. The second task involved focusing on eliminating mental and physical problems.

Not all of the work that Angelica did was 'serious'. She enjoyed interacting with children and animals and loved their positive and healthy Souls who had not yet forgotten who they were, tiny sparks of Divinity. One of the children she kept in touch with, and had agreed to be a Guide for, was 8-year-old Debbie. She loved her curiosity about all things related to Life. Why were we born? How did God unite the Soul and our body? What is Heaven like? What is the meaning of Death? Debbie was precocious and that made her more precious to Angelica. One time, while discussing world affairs, Angelica quoted John Muir's quote, "It is better to let live, than to kill." Debbie was so fascinated with this philosophy that she looked up John Muir on Wikipedia and was impressed that he was a scientist, besides being a good man!

She also had a different set of mentors to prepare her better to help clients. The week before she was to start her lessons with a new mentor, Akashi, she went to his teaching area to familiarize herself with the surroundings. She was given directions to find his teaching area: to the left of Mamma Cass's cauldron as you enter the Divine Field.

Lord Akashi resided in a meditation garden bordered by sculpted hedges on three sides and a river at the furthermost edge. Near the river was a weeping willow tree with leaves dripping down to create a shaded, secluded area with a beautiful stone bench. In front of this was a small pond with Koi fish. The garden was huge, full of plantings of all sizes and colors. There were flower beds and pathways paved in flagstone meandering through them. Throughout the garden were stools and benches and rocks for seating at strategic viewpoints.

There were colorful blooms filling the air with scent, plants with leaves which encourage the visitor to touch and beauty to look at from every angle. Everything was cultivated to stir the senses and stimulate the Sublime Mind while soothing the heart. Akashi, while very ancient, looked to be an attractive man in his late 20's, with Oriental facial features. He looked as if had just jumped out of a Manga graphic novel. He was tall and well dressed, radiating a sense of being ready to take on any challenge presented to him. He smiled, when she approached him. He used sense of calmness and peace to create an atmosphere conducive to creativity and possibility.

"Lord Akashi," Angelica bowed slightly as a sign of respect for the teacher.

Akashi bowed back, then hovered his right hand over her head to bless her. "I am humbled to know that Sensei has recommended that I take you under my tutelage. "

"It will be my honor if you can impart your wisdom to me,"

"I am ready if you are,"

Angelica nodded and bowed again.

***

The first lesson with Lord Akashi was to help Angelica regain the ability to feel like a human and bring her heart, soul, mind, and body back into harmony. This was supposed to be a transferable skill so that she could relay the ability to her clients and they could begin to manifest their best and highest good and their best life.

"Angelica, whether your clients choose to seek a spiritual life, one which reflects their Soul purpose, utilizes their spiritual gifts and allows them to be of service to see life, or not, manifesting is part of their daily practice. Manifesting is a healthy way to stay in tune with their chosen path and to maintain their own wholeness. But let's begin with what manifesting is not. It is not a way to coerce others, to control situations, to enact your will on others or to take away another's free will. In fact, proper manifestation must be done with an attitude of surrender to God and without mind power, involving our ego or willing something into being. Those perspectives come from a mindset of separation, of 'us' and 'them', of fear and lack."

This was a skill set, Angelica poured her heart and soul into as she knew Matt Quiggly needed this to revive his failing marriage and help him to shape the best family life he could give as a husband, dad, son and grandson.

White Angel

Gee Cii Schnider

There's a white angel out there

Out there somewhere

It'll blow away the darkness

Let is bright light shine

There's a white angel out there

With gold encrusted wings

A white halo of leaves

They only show certain people they're their angel

There's a white angel out there

One for each of us

Be they a friend to save you

Or a true being of Heaven

There's a white angel out there

Just let them find you please

They'll show you light

They'll save you from dark

There's a white angel out there

Just let them break through their darkness

Let them gain those wings

And you'll see them waiting

There's a white angel out there

Just you wait and see

CHAPTER 4: REUNION

Miranda had noticed a lot of change in Matt in the past few days. It was a good change, she had decided and felt relieved.

Sigh.

She was convinced that in a few months either he or she would have been making a decision to separate for a few months, had it not been for this recent positive change.

When Matt asked her to sit down with him when he came home from work, she was nervous, hoping their talk will help get their marriage on track.

"Mira. . . I need to share with you what has been on my mind lately," Matt quickly blurted out, paused and then looked into Miranda's eyes.

Miranda nodded to prompt him to continue and then put her right hand on his left knee and squeezed. She wanted to hear whatever he wanted to say. Spill it out. Like a bag of marbles, waiting to be spilled to the ground and admired in the light. She wasn't very confident if she would have the strength to listen to what he had to say, but she valued his expression in this form.

"I have been very disturbed by our distancing for the past several months. Couldn't put a finger on what were the factors that were driving us apart. Did you notice that?"

"Yes." Miranda said and hung her head down then quickly raised it, "I was very disturbed by it too, hoping you would find a way out to reach back to me." A tear spilled off her eye and made a splash mark on her jeans. Matt rubbed the wet spot as if regretting that he didn't stop it before it was spilled.

"Well, I was hoping you would do the same for me. Maybe, in the hoping and waiting, our gulf got wider and wider."

Miranda's bitter smile made him feel more guilty, "I tried, Matt but I felt I couldn't reach you. You would withdraw into your shell each time I tried to talk or touch."

Matt felt like he was coming back to consciousness after being in an emotional coma for several months. "Did I really do that?" He questioned himself.

"Matt, I am grateful that you and I are having this conversation. I was thinking that our marriage will be part of the sad statistic that says that 62% of marriages fail before their 15th anniversary."

"I promise I will do whatever we need. . . no, whatever what *I* need to do to get our relationship back like it was, based on mutual love."

"Why don't we start with spending more time with each other?" Miranda said and looked for signs of sincerity in Matt's eyes. She was relieved when they shone brighter.

"I was hoping you will suggest something so I can say yes. I wanted you to throw me the rope and reel me in, honey." and threw his muscular arms around Miranda to draw her to himself.

Miranda felt warmth leaping onto her heart to melt any icy cold spots. But she was not completely convinced that their marriage was safely on track and moving forward, full force, yet. She hated the term 'time heals' but surrendered to it as it popped up in her mind.

***

It was the third day after their talk and they were getting ready to go on a date, but the babysitter, the next door neighbor Mrs. Smith was late.

"Billy is very fussy," Miranda said while putting on mascara.

"I'll call Mrs. Smith to find out what's keeping her....Oh, there she is!" Matt felt relieved when the door rang.

Miranda rushed to open the door.

"I am so sorry, Mira," Mrs. Smith rushed in, hugged Miranda, "my daughter called from Virginia. She and grandkids are coming in this weekend. . . I am so sorry I kept you waiting."

Miranda shrugged and said, "That's good that Mimi is coming over next week." She grabbed her coat and stepped out with Matt.

It felt unusual to go out on a date after such a long time. She slipped her hand in his and it felt right. He tightened his grip on her hand and it felt great. That's what she needed again: reassurance that if she took a step to be close to him that he would double his effort to get close to her.

When they got to the restaurant, it was packed and they couldn't get in. Miranda shrugged her shoulders. "Let's just go for a walk?" she suggested and he nodded. The sky was clear and dotted with sparkling stars. She loved the night air and breathed it deep in her lung. Matt followed her gaze and copied her and both laughed.

"You have no idea how grateful I am for you, Mira." Matt planted a kiss on her hand and held it in his hands, cupping it as if protecting it.

"I am grateful for you too, Matt. I was very worried about us, watching our sense of intimacy crumble bit by bit as we pretended to be silent spectators."

Matt nodded.

"Matt, do you remember how we used to go to the church together? Rory used to love that. Can we start doing that again?

Matt hesitated. In the past, Miranda being Jewish, she had asked Matt to accompany him to her synagogue. Miranda was worried he would say no. Then he nodded his head. "Yes, I think that gave us an excellent reason to do stuff together. After church, we would invite new people we would meet at the church to have lunch with us. We had a bigger circle of friends as well. Let's do that this Sunday."

Not exactly what Miranda wanted to hear but she was hopeful that but if they both tried to put God in the middle of their relationship, their marriage would be a lot healthier than it had been in the past few months.

"How about that Chinese place, China Wall? You hungry now?"

"Yes, I am getting there. Their Rangoons are to die for."

"Let's go get them then!" Matt yelled and almost pulled her with him, making Miranda squeal with delight. It felt like being in High School again. No worries, no money, but still be able to have fun.

***

Next morning, Matt woke up a bit late but he felt it was worth it. He was regaining his best friend in life back. The pain of knowing he was almost about to end this relationship was weighing heavy on his conscience, especially since Angelica had now become part of his business life. He still wasn't over the shock that she was not human, but he was grateful that she had turned his life around, just the way he wanted it to be.

CHAPTER 5: TROUBLED WATERS

When at the office, he called Angelica to verify some information regarding the project. He hated having to call her as each time he called it reminded him that he had made a fool of himself.

"Hi Matt! Good to hear your voice," Angelica's soft-spoken voice was like melted butter and maple syrup on pancakes.

"Good, and you?"

"Great. Are you calling to verify the EIN number?"

"Yeah"

"That is 52-7741098. Listen, I have some news to share regarding your missing Uncle John. Are you able to meet me at Biaggi's today at noon?

"Yeah, yeah. . .Sure."

"All right, I will be there."

***

Matt got to Biaggi's as usual, a few minutes earlier than planned. He was surprised to see Angelica had beat him to it this time. She had chosen a booth in the corner and waved to him when she saw him.

"Hey!"

"Hey, Matt," she waved to him to sit down and seemed impatient. He focused on her eyes and raised his eyebrow as a question.

"I think I have the right person who could be your Uncle John."

Matt's heart started to race and felt tingling sensation all across his body. He got his face closer to her lips so he could hear better. Didn't want to miss anything over the din in the background.

"I have a friend in Malaysia, married to a Diplomat there. She faxed me these documents," Angelica pushed a large manila envelope.

Matt leaned forward to retrieve it and got the document out. He stared at the faded photo of an old man for a long time. He was certain that was the person his grandparents had been looking for what seemed like an eternity. Uncle John looked so much like Gram Pa, as his Stacy loved to call him. His eyes were pouring out hot, steaming tears. Angelica reached over and squeezed his arm gently to bring him back to reality. He nodded and wiped his eyes.

"How can we be sure this is Uncle John?" he looked at Angelica with beseeching eyes.

"I can't promise you that yet, but I think the evidence we have is strong enough to talk to your grandparents and share this." Matt choked up and tears threatened to emerge again. She wrapped her arms around him and he felt a bolt of energy enter his heart, giving him the courage to stand up and walk out of the restaurant.

Instead of going to his office, he decided to commute to his grandparent's house, an hour away from him. Now he was worried that he had not told his wife and made an arrangement to have their kids picked up from the school so he stopped at a gas station to use the pay phone, as his cell phone's battery had died.

"Sweetie!" he almost shouted making the people around him stop and turn in his direction. "Hon, I think I have some information about Uncle John so I am going to Gram Pa's house. Can you pick up the kids today?"

"That's great! Uhh, yes, I will be able to pick up the kids. I will just need to cancel Billy's pediatrician appointment."

After hanging up, he dialed Gram Pa's number to make sure they were home. Then he rushed to his truck to get back on the road. He wished he could just blink his eyes and be there to share the information. He could have mailed the photo but he wanted to see their reaction.

When he got there, Gram Ma, as his kids loved to call her was on the porch, pacing. Gram Pa was standing. Their faces looked stressed and grim. They had faced so much heartbreak since Uncle John went missing and they were bracing themselves for another blow to their hearts.

"I called your mom. She is inside."

Matt, without wasting any more time, pulled the photo fax and held it towards them. Gram Ma looked stunned, as if struck by lightning and unable to move or breathe. Gram Pa showed more sign of life and whispered "It's our boy, Ma" At the age of 85, Gram Pa's mind was as fast as a 30-year-old's. He might not be able to keep up with a marathon runner, but he led an active lifestyle and that helped him a lot. Matt's mom, Belinda, came rushing and hugged her parents and son, tears streaming down everyone's eyes. It was a bitter-sweet moment. All those years of trying and not being able to find him. So many questions racing in their minds.

Growing up, Matt's mom had given him little bits and pieces of information about her brother John Quigley who had been missing since September 15, 1945, that was 55 years ago. He was 12 years at that time and lied about his age when joining the Marines. So when found again, now he was 67 years old. Quigley's induction was on October 12, 1944, and it later became something of a scandal as it was revealed that the induction board which had drafted him had done so without a check into his background, based on verbal statements only from **Quigley** who had said that he was an orphan. The Marine Corps quietly discharged him on September 14, 1945, after only eleven months of service. The day later, he went missing.

"To say that John was a rebel would be an understatement. I was very young but I remember him giving Ma and Pa behavior trouble, at school the neighborhood, everywhere. Then he ran away and enlisted. It was as if he disowned us," she started crying and Matt rubbed her back. She straightened up and looked at her parents, "what's the next step now?" she managed to say between sobs.

"Can we call this lady who helped us find him? Should we fly to Malaysia, show up and surprise him?"

"I think we should fly there to meet him. I can get the address from the lady who helped us find him."

***

Matt decided to accompany all three to Malaysia to find Uncle John. According to Angelica's contact there, Uncle John lived in *Bukit Tunku*, the neighborhood of the ministers, royalties, etc, and owned an American-Oriental cuisine restaurant. He even had gotten married to a Malaysian lady and had two children, two boys. Gram Ma was very surprised. Matt's mom could hardly wait to hug him and meet his family.

Few days before the flight, all four made sure they were up to date on their vaccinations and as an extra precaution took alternative medicine to boost their immunity systems.

Gram Ma was really worried that what if he flat out denies they he knows them. Gram Pa tried to ease her mind by saying no point in worrying about it in advance.

Matt's mom packed pictures of him when he was young. He looked like Peter Pan, ready to leap into the next adventure. She worshiped him, and it broke her heart when she learned that she will not see him again. Now this streak of hope. She wanted it to lead her and her family to the reunion she had dreamed of as a little girl. She had prayed so sincerely to God to help her brother come back home. Doesn't God respond to sincerity, she had often wondered as a little girl.

***

Matt tried calling Angelica from the airport as soon as him and his family got to Kuala Lumpur International Airport. He wanted to consult her on a few things. His call couldn't go throw as 'all lines were busy'. He decided to join his family to retrieve the luggage. Retrieving it was hassle-free and then made their way towards the airport entrance to look for a taxi service. There were not a lot of taxis available, but they were surprised to see a placard with "Quiggly Family" on it written in big and bold handwriting. Matt waved and pointed to his family and shouted, "Are you looking for us? We are the Quiggly family."

The man came closer and he had an interesting mix of American and Orintal facial features. "Hello, I am Bobby Quiggly," he extended his hand and shook his head.

"Are you John's son?" Matt's mother couldn't wait any longer.

"Yes, John is my father and he sent me to get you from the airport."

"How did you know we are coming?"

"Our friend and neighbor told us that she had been in contact with a friend in

America and that they are coming here to meet Dad."

"Not just John, but his family too," Gram Ma stepped forward and hugged Bobby. "I am your Grandmother, child." Gram Pa joined his wife in hugging his grandson. Then Matt and his mom followed.

"Dad is waiting, let's get going." Everyone piled into a big tan colored Suzuki Van painted as what appeared to be promoting a restaurant. They already had hotel rooms reserved before they came to Malaysia, but Bobby insisted they stay at his home.

The drive from the airport to the neighborhood was 45 minutes long. Everyone wanted to talk but were afraid to disturb the silence.

When they got to the house, they saw Uncle John waiting for them in the front yard. Matt didn't expect this at all. Actually, the whole family was thinking there might be a confrontation waiting for them. Instead, Uncle John almost ran to

Gram Pa. Gram Ma came up behind them and hugged Uncle John, with tears streaming down her cheeks. "John, we waited so long for this moment."

"Ma, Pa, I really regret causing you two so much heartache. Now as a father, I know what I must have put you through. Can you please forgive me?" his eyes were welling up and voice was shaky.

Gram Pa nodded and hugged. Matt knew Gram Pa will not say anything right now as the pain of losing their son was decades-long as compared to seconds-long joy of finding a son.

The Guardian-Angel
Robert Browning

I.

Dear and great Angel, wouldst thou only
leave
That child, when thou hast done with him,
for me!
Let me sit all the day here, that when eve
Shall find performed thy special ministry,
And time come for departure, thou,
suspending
Thy flight, mayst see another child for
tending,
Another still, to quiet and retrieve.

II.

Then I shall feel thee step one step, no
more,
From where thou standest now, to where I
gaze,
---And suddenly my head is covered o'er
With those wings, white above the child
who prays
Now on that tomb---and I shall feel thee
guarding
Me, out of all the world; for me, discarding
Yon heaven thy home, that waits and opes
its door.

III.

I would not look up thither past thy head
Because the door opes, like that child, I
know,
For I should have thy gracious face instead,
Thou bird of God! And wilt thou bend me
low
Like him, and lay, like his, my hands
together,
And lift them up to pray, and gently tether

Me, as thy lamb there, with thy garment's
spread?

IV.

If this was ever granted, I would rest
My bead beneath thine, while thy healing
hands
Close-covered both my eyes beside thy
breast,
Pressing the brain, which too much thought
expands,
Back to its proper size again, and smoothing
Distortion down till every nerve had
soothing,
And all lay quiet, happy and suppressed.

V.

How soon all worldly wrong would be
repaired!
I think how I should view the earth and
skies
And sea, when once again my brow was
bared

Angel

After thy healing, with such different eyes.
O world, as God has made it! All is beauty:
And knowing this, is love, and love is duty.
What further may be sought for or
declared?

VI.

Guercino drew this angel I saw teach
(Alfred, dear friend!)---that little child to
pray,
Holding the little hands up, each to each
Pressed gently,---with his own head turned
away
Over the earth where so much lay before
him
Of work to do, though heaven was opening
o'er him,
And he was left at Fano by the beach.

VII.

We were at Fano, and three times we went
To sit and see him in his chapel there,
And drink his beauty to our soul's content

---My angel with me too: and since I care
For dear Guercino's fame (to which in
power
And glory comes this picture for a dower,
Fraught with a pathos so magnificent)---

VIII.

And since he did not work thus earnestly
At all times, and has else endured some
wrong---
I took one thought his picture struck from
me,
And spread it out, translating it to song.
My love is here. Where are you, dear old
friend?
How rolls the Wairoa at your world's far
end?
This is Ancona, yonder is the sea.

CHAPTER 6: SECOND REUNION

Uncle John decided to fly his whole family, wife and two sons and their wives and kids to Colorado to officially 'come home' to Gram Ma and Gram Pa.

Matt and Miranda needed to make sure there was space for all the family. They decided to take in Bobby Quiggly and his family stay at their home. They had a large loft with two rooms and a full bathroom, which would be perfect for Bobby's family of two adults and two kids. They had one queen bed in the loft so they decided to buy an air mattress for Bobby's kids who were a 12-year-old daughter and a 5-year-old son.

Gram Ma and Gram Pa were busy too and had hired a temporary housekeeper to help with cleaning and getting the two bedrooms ready to receive Uncle John and his wife and his older son Mike Quiggly, Mike's wife and one son, who was 15 years-old.

They were going to stay for 2 and a half months, so it was Matt's responsibility to create an itinerary to suit everyone's interests. He had planned for trips to local science museums for the kids, festivals and a trip to Grand Canyon for the whole family. He also decided to reserve a RV that could sleep 13 people.

The kids had come prepared with homework given by their school teachers to make sure they do not lag behind in studies while traveling. Matt's three were having a great time learning about Malaysian culture and language.

Uncle John had tried to pay for the RV, but Matt threatened to not talk to him if he did let him take care of him like his family.

Thanksgiving was two weeks away so Matt and Miranda decided to celebrate the Thanksgiving at Gram Pa's house.

"Allow me to cook the Turkey," Miranda pleaded with Gram Ma and she was grateful to have the task off her list. Miranda really loved preparing for Thanksgiving, enjoying decorating with warm and vibrant colors of the Fall and also make her recipes colorful with orange, purple, red and yellow hues. Her friends called her the culinary artist and she took this responsibly very seriously. In fact, she also had a 4-year degree as a professional chef and had thought about pursuing Masters in Restaurant Management.

"I'll be deep frying two birds, ok? I can also bring in green bean casserole and pecan pie." Being from North Carolina, she loved her Southern background and wasn't shy to influence her culinary talents.

"Are you sure you can manage all that?"

"Yes, I am very sure I can manage that, Mom." she turned around to face Matt's mom.

"You are such a darling, child." Matt's mom hugged Miranda. "I can bring mashed potatoes, fried, stuffed mushrooms and sparkling apple cider. Please remind Matt that John's family doesn't drink, ok?"

Miranda nodded.

On the day of the Thanksgiving, Uncle John and his family were grateful to be part of the family, enjoying the bounty.

"*Selamat petang,*" Matt's son, Rory blurted out, before his shyness made him clam up. he smiled mischievously. Matt, tugged at his cheek. Uncle John's wife, Aishah wrapped her arms around him, "You speak very good Malay. What is your name?"

"Rory!" he was enjoying this attention, being the middle child that he was.

"Well Rory, I really love your house. Can you teach me the names of these wonderful dishes?"

Everyone sat down and started enjoying each other's company as if they had known each other for ages. Uncle John was relieved, but very nervous about the possibility of being confronted by his Father. Whether you are 4 or 90, a dad is a dad and his reprimand and questioning can be nerve-wrecking at any age. "Well, I

better enjoy this before I have to face him,"
he thought.

My Angel

Ernestine Northover

An angel floated overhead,
With such soft gentle eyes,
I lay entranced upon my bed,
'Is this like when one dies? ',
The notion flashed quick through my
mind,
How was it she was here,
Why was she hovering, I was inclined,
To ask, but I in fear
Did not have courage to move or
speak,
I seemed completely dumb,
There was no way that I could seek
An answer, I felt too numb.
She spread her wings and flew away,
The mists rolled in above,
And I sensed that I just had to pray,
My heart was filled with love.
I raised my head and looked around,
And then suddenly I knew
It was a dream and with awareness,

found
My angel had been you!

CHAPTER 7: NEW CHALLENGE

When Matt drove Uncle John and his family to the airport, Uncle John hugged and put a small box in his hand. "Open it when you get home."

Matt opened it as soon as he got home that day and he found a gold key chain with several religious symbols; cross, Buddha statue, green crescent with a star and a star of David. Matt knew why he was given this as a gift and was grateful for having an Uncle that was so accepting of other's cultures and people of other faiths.

He made a note in his calendar to call Angelica when he got to the office the next day.

***

"Thank you for calling Leightly Media, how may I direct your call?" Matt was surprised to find a new voice greeting him.

"Oh, hi. Is Ms. Anjelica there?

"Sorry, Mr. Quiggly, she no longer works for us."

"Was she fired?"

"No, she resigned a month ago to pursue a new opportunity."

"Did she leave any contact details?"

"No."

Matt had come to a dead end. He couldn't help but get back into his busy and lively family life. "Maybe that was the main purpose of Angelica coming into my life," he often wondered.

***

The truth was that Angelica was called back to her regular duties on the other side of the country where she cared for a young, but confused, couple.

Minor physical ailments along with many emotional traumas had left the couple vulnerable to lots of physical, emotional and spiritual pain. Angel helped them greatly with chair exercises, love, and gave them true grit. This happened by Reiki-style, 'laying on the hands.'

"Emma, I don't know how I can go on with this. . ." Bradley put his right hand on his back and looked towards his wife with a painful look.

"I know, Sweetie, I too cannot live with this excruciating pain," she put her hand on her right lower tummy, where cyst had formed and threatened to derail her, not only her wonderful career, but also her whole life.

Both in their late twenties, they had very lucrative careers. Emma owned her bridal boutique, Bouquet, while Bradley was a Sales Executive at a software company and worked from home.

***

When these clients were assigned to Angelica, she started with accessing their Book of Life first.

Accessing the Book was an easy and quick way to download her client's life experiences and the emotions that they had associated with their experiences.

It didn't use to be that easy, until Aaroon showed her how to focus on the interactive part of the book on the left and use the textual part on the right as a guide, if she got stuck in interpreting her clients' lives. Now, she rarely had to consult the textual part. Besides, it was more fun to interact with the holographic account of her clients' lives, seeing what happened to them with their eyes; she literally got to be in their shoes. No better way to be an empath, one of the greatest tool in her kit of diversified skills.

Now she was ready to jump into the next adventure of helping another couple.

Touched By An Angel

Maya Angelou

unaccustomed to courage
exiles from delight
live coiled in shells of loneliness
until love leaves its high holy temple
and comes into our sight
to liberate us into life.

Love arrives
and in its train come ecstasies
old memories of pleasure
ancient histories of pain.
Yet if we are bold,
love strikes away the chains of fear
from our souls.

We are weaned from our timidity
In the flush of love's light
we dare be brave
And suddenly we see
that love costs all we are
and will ever be.
Yet it is only love
which sets us free.

www.ingramcontent.com/pod-product-compliance
Lightning Source LLC
Chambersburg PA
CBHW071539100726
47908CB00004B/1439